# Princess Rosa's Winter

## JUDY HINDLEY

### Illustrated by
# MARGARET CHAMBERLAIN

Kingfisher

02703

KINGFISHER

An imprint of Kingfisher Publications Plc
New Penderel House, 283-288 High Holborn
London WC1V 7HZ

First published by Kingfisher 1997
4 6 8 10 9 7 5
Text copyright © Judy Hindley 1997
Illustrations copyright © Margaret Chamberlain 1997

Educational Adviser: Prue Goodwin
Reading and Language Centre
University of Reading

A CIP catalogue record for this book
is available from the British Library.

ISBN 1 85697 491 X

Printed in Singapore

# *Contents*

# Chapter One

It was a winter morning

long ago.

Inside the castle,

it was dark and cold.

When Princess Rosa first woke up,

the candle by her bed

was still alight.

Princess Rosa asked her nurse,

"Why is it so dark

when we wake up?"

Nurse Bonny said to her,

"Because it's winter.

The sun does not get up

till very late, now.

Winter is a dark time."

Nurse Bonny blew on the fire

to make it blaze.

But when the small princess

jumped out of bed,

she still felt cold.

She put on

one gown

over

another –

but she still felt cold!

She said,

"It is too cold, today!

Why is it so cold?"

Nurse Bonny said,

"Because it's winter.

The sun is tired

and the snow is falling.

A dark world is a cold world."

Rosa huddled with her
dogs beside the fire.
Nurse Bonny
toasted bread
and warmed some beer.
Every morning,
breakfast was the same –
but they ate every scrap.

Then they put on their
cloaks and hurried off
to say good morning
to the King and Queen.
Icy breezes whistled
down the hallway.
Cold, white mist
crawled along the
floor.

It was so cold,
the King and Queen
were still in bed.
"Climb up here,
my little climbing Rose!"
the King called out.
"Come and kiss me,
my sweet Rosa!"
cried the Queen.
So she did.
The royal bed had a roof
and curtains.
Inside, it was like a big,
warm cave.
It was very snug.

But here came

the King's Chief Steward

to tell the King

about important business.

And here came

the Lord High Chancellor

to ask the King

a very important question.

And here came the priest

to say a prayer

with the Queen.

And here came her maid

to fix her hair.

And here came the cook
with a big tray of breakfast,
and a little page-boy
with a message.

The doors were guarded
by the royal men-at-arms.
But the cat sneaked past,
and the royal dogs barked,
and finally, the King said,
"Enough!
Everyone must go!"
So they did.

# Chapter Two

Off went the princess
and her nurse, and her dogs.
Along the misty hallway,
down a twisty stair.

Out they went
through the great doors
of the castle.
But outside,
big, wet flakes of snow
were falling.

It was too cold
to take the dogs out
for a run.

It was too cold
to take the pony
for a ride.

It was so cold
the falcon
wouldn't fly.

They couldn't even feed
the ducks and fish.
The fish were hidden
underneath the ice.
The ducks and geese and
swans had gone away.
The small princess was cold.

Back they went
through the great doors
of the castle.
It was dinner-time.
Everyone gathered
in the great hall,
and a big fire blazed.
But everyone was gloomy.

For weeks and weeks,

they had not heard

one bit of news,

or one new song

or one new joke.

Everyone was bored.

When dinner came,

they were gloomier than ever.

21

"Same old thing again!"

said Princess Rosa.

"Can't I have an egg?"

"Oh, my darling,

there are no eggs in winter,"

said the Queen.

"When the days are dark,

the hens don't lay them."

The small princess

threw down her spoon.

She cried,

"I don't like winter!"

"Hush!" said Nurse Bonny.

"Winter has some good things."

"Name one,"

said Princess Rosa.

Everyone thought hard.

"I'm sure there are
*some* good things,"
said the old knight.

"I know!"
cried the little page-boy.

"Snow!

It is good for sleds
and good for sliding,
and it is great for snow-balls."

"Christmas!" said the Queen.

"Christmas is a wonderful winter thing.

We all dress up

and we dress up the castle

with ribbons and little bells

and boughs of greenery and berries.

Then we dance

while the minstrels play for us."

Princess Rosa said,

"Snow is cold.

I don't know if I like it.

I don't know if I like dressing-up

or dancing.

I still think winter is no good."

But the King said,

"There is one good thing

that nobody has mentioned.

Hode."

"What is Hode?"

asked Princess Rosa.

But just then,

CRASH!

The castle doors flew open.

WHOOOO!

The winter wind

came whirling in.

# Chapter Three

There in the doorway

stood a huge, white, furry creature.

Everyone went quiet.

The furry creature

marched up

through the hall,

dripping snow.

The wind roared.

The fire crackled.

The drips of melted snow

said, "Hisss!"

The creature kneeled
before the King and Queen,
bowing low.

Then it stood up.

It shook off the snow.

It threw off the bear-skin.

"It's Hode!" cried the King.

"It's our wonderful winter visitor."

"It's Hode!" cried the Queen

and the knights

and men-at-arms.

"It's Hode!" cried the ladies,

and the servants,

and the fiddlers.

"Hurrah!" cried everyone.

"Hurrah!"

Hode was dressed from head to toe
in coloured patches,
and covered from head to toe
with bells and mirrors.
When he moved,
he glinted and he glittered
and he jingled.
From his sleeve
popped a ball
and then another
and another.
Soon, all the balls
were in the air.

He juggled them high
he juggled them low
he juggled them round his arms
and legs
and body.

He whistled them
into his hat
and out his sleeve
and back!

And then he did eleven somersaults
and thirteen back flips.
When he finished,
everyone clapped
and shouted.

"Hurrah!" cried everyone,
"Hurrah!"

The King was so excited,

he could not stop

giving orders.

He cried,

"Bring a bowl of apples!

Bring some walnuts!

Bring some chestnuts!

Bring the fiddles!

Bring some good red wine

for us to drink!

It's time to celebrate!"

"Indeed," said the Queen,

"Why wait for Christmas?"

Soon,

everyone was dancing

42

and all the long, dark winter night

they danced and played.

Very late that night,

when the little princess

went to bed

the snow had stopped.

Her nurse opened the shutter

just a crack

and they peeped out.

The moon was huge and white.

The bright snow gleamed

almost as bright as daylight.

"The snow is beautiful,"

said Princess Rosa.

"And Hode is wonderful,"
she said.

"And dancing is fun!"
she added.

"Ah," said the little princess,
"I can't wait till Christmas!"

## About the Author and Illustrator

**Judy Hindley** lives near an ancient forest in a town built in the time of knights and castles. Judy says, "I like winter because it's one of the best and cosiest times for reading books."

**Margaret Chamberlain** is interested in how people lived long ago. She says, "Life must have been hard. The seasons really ruled people's lives. But, as Princess Rosa finds out, they also had a lot of fun!"

If you've enjoyed reading *Princess Rosa,*
try these other **I Am Reading** books:

ALLIGATOR TAILS AND CROCODILE CAKES
Nicola Moon & Andy Ellis

BARN PARTY
Claire O'Brien & Tim Archbold

GRANDAD'S DINOSAUR
Brough Girling & Stephen Dell

KIT'S CASTLE
Chris Powling & Anthony Lewis

MISS WIRE AND THE THREE KIND MICE
Ian Whybrow & Emma Chichester Clark

MR COOL
Jacqueline Wilson & Stephen Lewis

WATCH OUT, WILLIAM
Kady MacDonald Denton